JONATHAN JASPER JEREMY JONES

By Bernice C. Holland
Illustrated by Duane Hoffmann

Other Books by Storytellers Ink

A Bug C
Beautiful Joe
Black Beauty
Bustop the Cat
Cousin Charlie the Crow
Father Goose & His Goslings
If a Seahorse Wore a Saddle
I Thought I Heard a Tiger Roar
Kitty the Raccoon
Little Annie of Christian Creek
Lobo the Wolf
Monica the Monarch Butterfly
Not For Sadie
Ragglylug the Cottontail Rabbit
Redruff the Partridge of Don Valley
Sandy of Laguna
Sully the Seal and Alley the Cat
The Adventures of J.G. Cougar
The Blue Kangaroo
The Living Mountain
The Lost & Found Puppy
The Pacing Mustang
Tweak and the Absolutely Right Whale
William's Story

Jonathan Jasper Jeremy Jones
was a busy young fellow without any bones.
He was born one day in an apple tree
and thought the world was what he could see.

"My this world is a beautiful green
and good to eat, that's plain to be seen."
He ate and ate so he could grow.
He ate the leaves of his house, and so....

When he lifted his head and looked around
he was delighted to see the ground.
"The world is bigger than just this tree.
I really must go down and see."

So Jonathan Jasper Jeremy Jones
a curious fellow without any bones,
went humping and bumping and inching along.
His idea was good but his path was wrong.

For while he was humping along a limb,
danger was waiting to strike at him.
A hungry robin with beady eye,
saw fat, fuzzy Jonathan creeping by.

The robin swooped into the tree
and Jonathan gasped "It's the end for me."
But just as the robin's beak came around
Jonathan let go and dropped to the ground.

He hid in the grass for part of the day
until it seemed safe to crawl away.
"This world is so big and I'm so small
I'm afraid I don't count for much at all."

Jonathan Jasper Jeremy Jones,
a determined young fellow without any bones,
pulled himself up to the top of a stone,
hoping that he would be left alone.

But down in the grass where Jon couldn't see,
a snake was thinking, "There's lunch for me."
He slithered along and was coming quite near
when Jonathan noticed and shook with fear.

The snake was getting ready to bite
when Jonathan twisted with all his might.
The snake struck but his fangs went wide
as Jonathan Jasper rolled to the side.

Jonathan Jasper Jeremy Jones,
that frightened young fellow without any bones,
went humping and bumping through fields of grass,
till he came to a road that looked hard to pass.

Tractors and trucks were zooming through
and Jonathan hardly knew what to do.
Till one of them stopped and started to spray
the very tree he had left that day.

Lucky for him he went to explore,
since that tree wasn't healthy for him anymore.
And now he knew he must keep on going
even though the traffic was flowing.

Jonathan Jasper Jeremy Jones
that lucky young fellow without any bones,
scurried and scampered, and scooted and tried
to move safely across to the other side.

It took so long for him to crawl;
could he ever get through this world at all?
He thought about wings, he thought about speed.
"Wings, now that's what I really need."

Then Jonathan Jasper Jeremy Jones,
that weary young fellow without any bones,
said, "I'm getting so tired I need to rest.
I'll look for a place to build a nest."

He fastened his silk to a branch off the ground
and wrapped himself around and around.
He went to sleep the whole winter through,
and while he slept his wish came true.

Slowly within his tiny space
a wonderful change was taking place.
And one spring day in the warming sun
Jon woke up with work to be done.

"I must be up and on my way.
I can't lie around this cocoon all day."
So he wiggled his way into the air
and rested awhile, just hanging there.

And when his eyes had opened wide,
a most beautiful thing was by his side.
It was a butterfly, bold and free,
who said, "Jonathan, come fly with me."

"Why I can only hump and crawl.
I never could do that at all."
"Jon, you're not a caterpillar anymore.
Look at your wings, you're ready to soar."

So Jonathan Jasper Jeremy Jones,
An astonished young fellow without any bones,
looked at his wings in sheer delight
and rose on the air in perfect flight.

Bernice C. Holland (1907 - 1992) was a
beloved kindergarten teacher who wrote
this tender and happy story to involve her
students in the magic of spring.